CALCULATIN

"ONE, TWO, THREE, SIX!"

yelled Connie furiously.

Suddenly the truth dawned upon Mrs Button.

"She's right. Don't you see? She's not just counting.

She's adding."

ROLLO THE RHYMER

Rollo's mum and dad looked at one another.

"Do you notice . . ." whispered his mother.

"That everything he says . . ." murmured his father.

"Rhymes!" they both cried.

Two terrific tales within one book!

★Also available in book and audio tape packs.

DICK KING-SMITH

Connie and Rollo

Illustrated by Judy Brown

CONNIE AND ROLLO
A YOUNG CORGI BOOK : 0 552 52795 5

First published in Great Britain by Doubleday,
a division of Random House Children's Books

PRINTING HISTORY
Doubleday edition published 1994
Young Corgi edition published 1995

7 9 10 8

Text copyright © Fox Busters Ltd, 1994
Illustrations copyright © Judy Brown, 1994

The right of Dick King-Smith to be identified as the Author of this
work has been asserted in accordance with the Copyright,
Designs and Patents Act 1988.

Young Corgi Books are published by Random House Children's Books,
61–63 Uxbridge Road, London W5 5SA,
a division of The Random House Group Ltd,
in Australia by Random House Australia (Pty) Ltd,
20 Alfred Street, Milsons Point, Sydney, NSW 2061, Australia,
in New Zealand by Random House New Zealand,
18 Poland Road, Glenfield, Auckland 10, New Zealand
and in South Africa by Random House (Pty) Ltd,
Endulini, 5a Jubilee Road, Parktown 2193, South Africa.

Printed and bound in Great Britain by
CPI Antony Rowe, Chippenham and Eastbourne

CONTENTS

CALCULATING

CONNIE

Chapter 1

Connie Button seemed a very ordinary baby.

Not to Mr and Mrs Button, of course – they thought she was the most wonderful baby ever, as parents do.

Which she was, though at first they didn't know it.

When Connie was about eighteen months old, she still had not spoken a proper word. She made noises, of course, as babies do, but they didn't make sense.

Mr and Mrs Button were eagerly looking forward to the moment when she would say something that they could understand.

"Harold!" said Mrs Button one fine day, when her husband came home from work. "It's happened!"

"What has happened, Muriel?" asked Mr Button.

"Connie has spoken her very first word!"

"I say! What fun! What was it?" said Mr Button.

"'One'."

"One what?"

"That's what she said. She said, 'One'. That was her very first word."

"I say! That's odd," said Mr Button. "I wonder what she will say next."

Some weeks later, Mr Button arrived home to be told that Connie had spoken her second word.

"And what was it?" he asked.

"'Two'."

"She said, 'Two'?"

"Yes," said Mrs Button. "And then, what do you think? She said, 'One, two'."

"I say!" said Mr Button. "That's odd. I wonder what she will say next."

You might perhaps guess that the third word which Connie Button spoke, a month or so later, was "Three". You'd be right, and indeed she then said, "One, two, three," as Mrs Button told her husband when he got home.

And for quite a long time that was all that the child said. But I doubt if you could guess what happened next, on Connie's second birthday.

Mrs Button was dandling Connie
on her knee.

Mr Button was drinking a cup of
tea.

Connie Button was saying, "One, two, three."

You might perhaps think that Connie was about to say, "Four."

You'd be wrong.

Connie swallowed a mouthful of birthday cake, and then, loudly and clearly, she said, "One, two, three, six."

"No, Connie," said Mrs Button. "It's one, two, three, four."

"Is not!" said Connie.

"It is," said Mrs Button.

Connie Button's little face went very red. She clenched her fists and drummed angrily upon her mother's knee.

"One, two, three, six!" she shouted.

"I say!" said Mr Button. "What a fuss. Why is she making such a fuss, Muriel? She cannot know what she has done wrong."

"ONE, TWO, THREE, SIX!!" yelled Connie furiously.

Suddenly the truth dawned upon Mrs Button.

"She's right, Harold," she said. "She's right. Don't you see? She's not just counting. She's adding."

She cuddled Connie and dried her tears.

"One and two and three make six. That's what she's trying to say, aren't you, darling. What a clever girl."

"I don't think I can believe that," said Mr Button. "Anyway, I don't know how the child has learned these numbers. Have you been teaching her?"

"No," said Mrs Button. "She just comes out with them."

"Seven, nine, sixteen," said Connie.

"You see?" said Mrs Button. "Seven plus nine equals sixteen."

"I say!" said Mr Button. "That's odd."

"Is not," said Connie. "Is even."

"Did you hear that?" said Mrs Button. "She knows the difference between even and odd numbers!"

"I can't believe it, Muriel," said Mr Button.

"Try her, Harold."

Mr Button addressed his little daughter.

"Ten," he said.

"Even," said Connie.

"Five."

"Odd."

"Add eight to three."

"Eleven."

"Add four to thirteen."

"Seventeen," said Connie.

"I say!" said Mr Button. "The child is a genius, Muriel. Only two years old and she can add four and thirteen correctly. She's a mathematical genius!"

"Perhaps she can do even better, Harold. Who knows?" said Mrs Button. "Try her with a harder sum."

Mr Button smiled. He took out his pocket calculator.

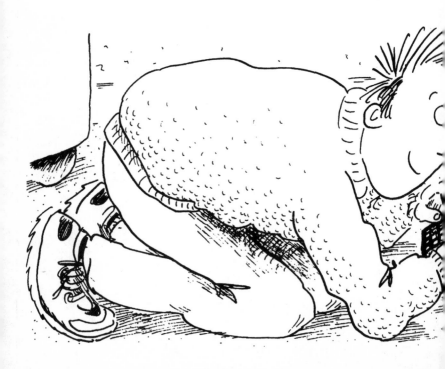

"She won't do this one in a hurry," he said. "Now then, Connie, listen carefully to Daddy and see if you can add these two numbers together. One thousand, three hundred and fifty-six plus . . ."

"Oh, Harold!" cried Mrs Button. "Don't be ridiculous!"

"It's only for a joke, Muriel," said Mr Button. "Of course she won't be able to do it. Listen then, Connie. One thousand, three hundred and fifty-six plus nine hundred and three."

Connie Button's little face wore a frown of concentration. She pursed her lips and stuck out the tip of her tongue and screwed up her eyes.

"Told you!" said Mr Button.

"Poor little love," said Mrs Button.

"Two thousand, two hundred and fifty-nine," said Connie Button.

Chapter 2

Mrs Button was doing her shopping, pushing Connie around the supermarket in a wire trolley. As she put the first item into it, Connie said, "One". Then the child continued to count, as the fish fingers and the disposable nappies and the bread and the margarine and all the other things were loaded up. Until, as they approached the checkout, Connie said, "Twenty-four", and Mrs Button thus knew that she had bought two dozen items.

The next time they went shopping, she said to herself, I'll try telling Connie the price of each thing as we go along, just for fun. You never know, she might be able to add them all up.

She picked up a bottle of tomato sauce and showed it to Connie and said, "This is forty-six pence,

Connie," and Connie nodded.

"There'll be lots more," said Mrs Button. "Can you add them all together for me?" and Connie nodded.

So up and down the aisles they went, while Mrs Button called out the prices as she loaded up the trolley.

"Tea – sixty-six pence," she said. "Biscuits – fifty-four pence. Tin of salt – thirty-eight pence. Small tin of chopped ham with pork – thirty-seven pence. Honey – one pound and fifty-nine pence." And so on till the trolley was full, and each time Connie just nodded.

"That's it, I think, Connie," Mrs Button said at last.

She'll never have remembered all that lot, poor little mite, she said to herself. That kind of mental arithmetic would be too hard for all but the cleverest of adults. Anyway, she was probably just nodding and not listening to what I said. But I can't resist asking.

As they moved towards the checkout, Mrs Button said, "How much altogether?"

"Seventeen pounds and twenty pence," said Connie.

Opening your purse with your

fingers crossed is not easy, but Mrs
Button managed it, and as the
checkout girl was starting to ring up
her purchases, she placed upon the
counter a ten pound note, a five
pound note, two pound coins and a
twenty pence piece.

"Seventeen pounds and twenty pence, please," said the checkout girl at last, and then realized that the exact money had been sitting there waiting.

"Fancy!" she said. "You add 'em up as you go along, do you?"

Mrs Button smiled. "My little daughter does," she said, and the checkout girl laughed loudly at so ridiculous an idea.

Whatever will Harold say when I tell him? thought Mrs Button. Apart from his first two words, I mean — I know what *they'll* be.

"I say!" said Mr Button when he was told. "D'you mean to tell me,

Muriel, that Connie added up all the things you bought, in her head, and came out with the correct answer?"

"Yes, Harold," said Mrs Button.

"And you bought a large number of different things?"

"Oh yes," said Mrs Button. "An awful lot – I don't know how many."

"Twenty-seven," said Connie.

"I say!" said Mr Button.

"And I'll tell you another thing, Harold," said Mrs Button. "Because I was looking carefully at the prices so as to tell Connie what they were, I found quite a lot of bargains and saved some money. About five per cent I should say."

"What's per cent?" said Connie.

"Well, Connie," said Mr Button. "When Mummy says she saved five per cent, it means she saved five pence in every pound. So she only had to pay out seventeen pounds and twenty pence instead of . . . let me work it out," and he put his hand in his pocket.

". . . eighteen pounds and ten pence," said Connie.

Mr Button took out his little machine and pressed its buttons. He shook his head in wonderment.

"Muriel," he said, "I don't need this thing any more. We have our own human pocket calculator."

Chapter 3

Not only adding, but subtracting,
dividing and multiplying came easily
to Connie, the Buttons soon
discovered.

Life became much simpler for them.

Thanks to Connie, Mrs Button always knew exactly what her household expenses were, while Mr Button, who ran a small business of his own, found his daughter's skill most useful. His bills and receipts, his investments, his income tax and VAT returns, were all child's play to Connie. She needed some help, of course, for though she knew her numbers, she could not yet read any words, but all her calculations were correct to the last decimal point. No computer could have done better.

How proud of her the Buttons were, at first.

"Just think," said her mother, "what she could be when she's grown up!"

"Professor Constance Button, the world's greatest mathematician," said her father.

And they never tired of telling Connie how clever she was.

She might work out the price of curtain material – in her head, of course, as she could not manage a pencil – and Mrs Button would say, "That's brilliant!"

Or she might tot up a long list of different purchases, plus VAT at seventeen and a half per cent, and Mr Button would say, "Fantastic!"

At first Connie basked in all this praise, but as time went on and the Buttons grew accustomed to her feats of mental arithmetic, they began to accept her answers without comment.

"One hundred and forty-three pounds and thirty-five pence plus seventy-two pounds and six pence plus one hundred and seven pounds and three pence plus forty-two pounds and sixteen pence, less ten per cent," Mr Button said one day.

"Three hundred and twenty-eight pounds and fourteen pence," said Connie.

Mr Button wrote down the answer.

Connie looked sulky. "Naughty Daddy," she said. "Didn't say Connie was clever."

"Didn't I?" said Mr Button absently.

Connie stamped her foot. "Connie

cleverer than Daddy," she said.

"I say!" said Mr Button.

That was only the start of it, for Connie Button, it soon became plain to her parents, was becoming very swollen-headed.

"That's easy!" she took to saying whenever she was asked to do a sum, and that led to "Can't you do that yourself?" and that led to "Silly Mummy" and "Stupid Daddy".

Connie, in fact, began to patronize her parents, and, as well as being rude, she became disobedient and extremely bad-tempered.

"I say, Muriel," said Mr Button one

evening after Connie had gone to bed. "This is beginning to get me down. Do you know, I questioned one of Connie's answers today — I thought she had made a mistake and so I worked it out on my calculator. But, in fact, she had got it right."

"She would, wouldn't she, Harold?" said Mrs Button, and there was more than a trace of bitterness in her voice.

"But that's not all," said Mr Button. "I said to her, 'You were right,' and she said, 'Of course, I always am,' and d'you know, Muriel, I could have slapped the child, she looked so smug."

"And another thing," said Mrs Button. "She's taken to setting me problems. And if I try to write the sums down, she says, 'No, no, do it in your head, can't you? I can do it in mine.' It makes me feel such a fool, Harold."

"Me too, Muriel," said Mr Button.

At that moment, Connie appeared.

"Can't sleep," she said grumpily.

"Try counting sheep," said Mrs Button.

"How many?" said Connie.

"Count to a hundred."

"That's much too easy."

"A thousand then."

"That won't take long."

"Oh, count to a zillion," said Mr Button.

Connie looked scornfully at her father.

"Silly Daddy!" she said. "A zillion isn't a real number. You're stupid, you

are," and she flounced out of the room and up the stairs.

"I say!" said Mr Button. "I'm not putting up with any more of this," and

he shouted loudly, "Connie! Come back here!"

Now whether Connie turned suddenly when she heard her father's angry voice or whether she just missed her footing, we shall never know, but the next thing the Buttons heard was a thumpety-thumpety-thump as Connie Button tumbled all the way down the stairs from top to bottom, to lie spreadeagled upon the hall floor, senseless.

By the time the doctor arrived,
Connie seemed to have quite
recovered.

The doctor examined her.

"She's had a bit of a bang here," he
said, feeling her head.

"Mummy," said Connie. "Can I have an apple?"

"Ah!" said the doctor, smiling. "An apple a day keeps the doctor away. How many apples would that be each week, Connie, eh?"

Connie did not reply.

The doctor laughed.

"She's much too young to know her numbers, of course!" he said.

"I say!" said Mr Button, but then he caught his wife's eye and didn't say any more.

They waited until the doctor had gone, and then they looked at one another again.

"You heard what the doctor said, Muriel," said Mr Button.

"I did, Harold," said Mrs Button. "Wouldn't it be a relief though if Connie couldn't calculate?"

"And wasn't always right."

"And always able to do sums that we can't."

"And always saying, 'Silly Mummy'."

"Or 'Stupid Daddy'."

"In fact," said Mr Button, "if she was just an ordinary two year old."

They looked at Connie, playing happily with her toys.

"Try her with an easy sum,

Harold," said Mrs Button.

"Connie," said Mr Button. "What's five times nine?"

"Twenty-ten," said Connie.

Mr Button held up four fingers of one hand.

"Connie," he said. "What have I got here?"

"Fingers," said Connie.

"Yes, but how many?"

"One two three four eight six ten," said Connie.

"I say!" said Mr Button. "That doesn't sound like the future Professor Constance Button, the world's greatest mathematician."

"I know!" said Mrs Button. "Isn't it lovely! She's just like any other child of her age. After all, you're only two, aren't you, Connie?"

Connie smiled happily at her parents.

"Yes," she said.

"And when you have your next birthday," said her father, "how old will you be then?"

Connie Button's little face wore a frown of concentration. She pursed her lips and stuck out the tip of her tongue and screwed up her eyes. Then she gave a huge smile.

"Four!" she cried, and all three Buttons burst out laughing.

ROLLO THE

RHYMER

Chapter 1

When Rollo was a baby, he looked quite ordinary.

He crawled about, and laughed and cried, and made funny noises just as all babies do.

Nobody noticed anything different about Rollo – until he started to speak.

The first words he said, when his mother had given him a biscuit and he had eaten it, were:

"ANOTHER,
MOTHER."

Nothing special about that, you might say, but that same evening his father, helping with the washing-up, dropped a plate and broke it, and Rollo said:

"BAD
DAD."

His parents were proud, of course, that he had started to speak, and so clearly too. But the way in which he spoke did not strike them as unusual until a couple of months later.

They were watching their baby as he played on the bedroom floor, when suddenly he crawled out of the room, saying as he did so:

"FOLLOW
ROLLO."

Wondering, they did as they were told, and Rollo led them into the bathroom. On the floor beside the bath stood his pink plastic pot, and Rollo, pointing first to it and then slapping his nappied behind, said:

"BOTTY –
POTTY."

They took off his nappy and sat him on the pot, and he performed. Then he exclaimed triumphantly:

"ME

WEE."

His mum and dad looked at one another.

"Do you notice . . ." whispered his mother.

"That everything he says . . ." murmured his father.

"Rhymes!" they both cried.

"TOO

TRUE,"

said Rollo.

"Perhaps it's just a fluke?" they said to one another.

"NO, NO,

NOT SO,"

said Rollo, and then, as though to make sure they'd got the message, he said:

> "ROLLO RHYME
> ALL THE TIME."

Chapter 2

As Rollo grew bigger, his rhymes
grew longer. Now he was never
content with a simple "Yes" or "No".

At mealtimes, for example, if asked
whether he would like some more, he
might reply (nodding):

"SECOND HELPS FOR ROLLO.
FEELING RATHER HOLLOW."

Or (shaking his head):

"ROLLO FULL TO BRIM.
NOTHING MORE FOR HIM."

Of course, there was no way of keeping Rollo's rhymes a secret. Other members of the family, like grandparents and aunts and uncles and cousins, soon grew used to the way he talked.

"And how's little Rollo?" they

would say, and he might answer
(either):

"VERY WELL TODAY.
THANK YOU, AUNTIE MAY."

(Or perhaps):

"ROLLO GOT THE TUMMY ACHE,
ATE TOO MUCH OF GRANNY'S CAKE."

(Or if he was in a bad mood):

"PLEASE DO NOT CALL ME 'LITTLE',
UNCLE JOE.
IN CASE YOU HADN'T NOTICED
BABIES GROW."

And grow he did, so that soon it was time for him to go to school.

On his first day, the teacher asked him his name, and he replied:

"ROLLO IS MY NAME, OF COURSE.
CAN YOU TELL ME – WHAT IS YOURS?"

The teacher was so surprised that she simply said:

"My name is Miss Rice."
"THAT'S AWFULLY NICE,"
said Rollo.

Throughout the morning his replies to anything the teacher said to him all rhymed, and at lunchtime she went to tell the headmaster about it.

The headmaster summoned Rollo to his office and said, "Now what's all this, sonny? You trying to be funny?"

"OH SIR, HOW LOVELY! YOU'RE ANOTHER! JUST WAIT UNTIL I TELL MY MOTHER!"
cried Rollo.

The headmaster looked baffled, so Rollo went on:

> "I'M A
> RHYMER.
> ARE YOU
> ONE TOO?"

The headmaster shook his head in bewilderment, and when school ended and Rollo's mother came to collect her son, he asked her what was the matter with the boy. But then he wished he hadn't.

Rollo's way of speaking was catching, and by now his parents often spoke in the same way.

"Now one thing you must understand," said Rollo's mother to the headmaster. "His way of speaking is not planned. It's just a fact that all the time you'll find that Rollo talks in rhyme."

Chapter 3

Eventually, as boys do, Rollo grew up.
Always, however, he spoke in the
same manner.

For example, when he took his
driving test, the examiner sitting

beside him said, "Right then, young man. Off we go, and good luck," and Rollo replied:

"YOU'LL SEE, WHEN WE
ARE ON THE ROAD,
I UNDERSTAND THE
HIGHWAY CODE FROM A TO Z,
FROM FIRST TO LAST.

WHEN WE RETURN,
I SHALL HAVE PASSED."

And so he had.

Some years later, when Rollo proposed to his girlfriend, he did not, as others might, simply say, "Will you marry me?" but

"SINCE I LOVE YOU
AND YOU LOVE ME,
I'M HOPING THAT
YOU WILL AGREE
TO MARRY ME,
AND ALL MY LIFE
I'LL BE YOUR HUSBAND,
YOU MY WIFE."

And so they were.

Later still, the children came along. Rollo, of course, insisted that each should have rhyming names. There were two boys, Ronald Donald and Eric Derek, and three girls, Cora Flora Nora, Molly Polly Dolly and Letty Hetty Betty.

And later still, much later – for Rollo the Rhymer lived to a great old age – he passed peacefully away, surrounded by his family.

To no-one's surprise his last words, though brief, were still in rhyme.

"I'LL SAY GOODBYE,
IT'S TIME TO DIE."

And he did.

If ever you should come upon his gravestone, you will know for sure who made up what is written upon it. This is what it says:

BENEATH THIS NOBLE
BLOCK OF STONE
DOES RHYMING ROLLO
LIE ALONE.
IN ALL THE WORLD YOU
WILL NOT FIND
ANOTHER ONE OF
ROLLO'S KIND.
HE SPOKE, FOR BETTER
OR FOR WORSE,
FROM BABE TO BOY TO
MAN IN VERSE,
AND HERE, FOR ALL THE
REST OF TIME,
IS WRITTEN ROLLO'S
FINAL RHYME.